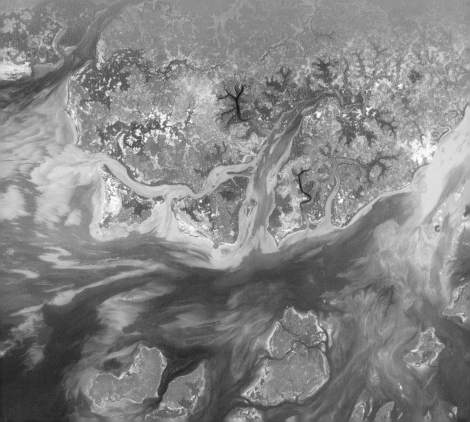

The Usborne
Little
Atlas

First published in this format in 2005 by Usborne Publishing Ltd,
Usborne House, 83–85 Saffron Hill, London EC1N 8RT, England.

www.usborne.com

Printed in Dubai.

Title page: A satellite image showing rivers joining the sea, along the coast of
Guinea-Bissau in west Africa. The red parts are land and the blue parts are water.
This page: These mountains and glaciers are on the island of Svalbard, which belongs
to Norway. The island is far inside the Arctic Circle and it's very cold there.

The Usborne
Little
Atlas

Elizabeth Dalby

Designed by Laura Hammonds,
Candice Whatmore and Ruth Russell

Additional design: Adam Constantine, Michael Hill,
Karen Tomlins, Joanne Kirkby and Luke Sargent

Digital imagery by Keith Furnival

Edited by Kirsteen Rogers

Cover design: Hannah Ahmed

Cartography: European Map Graphics Ltd

Consultant: John Davidson

Consultant cartographic editor: Craig Asquith

Website adviser: Lisa Watts

Using Internet links

Throughout this book we have suggested interesting websites where you can find out more about the different countries, customs, people and animals in this book. To visit the sites, go to the Usborne Quicklinks Website at **www.usborne-quicklinks.com** and type the keywords "first atlas". Here are some of the things you can do on the websites.

- Find exciting games and activites from Africa
- Discover the creatures living on a coral reef
- Visit the Eiffel Tower
- Explore a virtual European castle
- Take an Arctic quiz

Internet safety

When using the Internet, please make sure you follow these guidelines:

- Ask your parent's or guardian's permission before you connect to the Internet.
- If you write a message in a website guest book or on a website message board, do not include any personal information such as your full name, address or telephone number, and ask an adult before you give your email address.
- Never arrange to meet anyone you have talked to on the Internet.
- If a website asks you to log in or register by typing your name or email address, ask permission from an adult first.
- If you do receive an email from someone you don't know, tell an adult and do not reply to the email.

To go to all the websites that are described in this book, go to **www.usborne-quicklinks.com** and enter the keywords "first atlas".

Site availability

The links in Usborne Quicklinks are regularly reviewed and updated, but occasionally, you may get a message that a site is unavailable. This might be temporary, so try again later, or even the next day. Websites do occasionally close down and when this happens, we will replace them with new links in Usborne Quicklinks. Sometimes we add extra links too, if we think they are useful. So when you visit Usborne Quicklinks, the links may be slightly different from those described in your book.

Notes for parents and guardians

The websites described in this book are regularly reviewed and the links in Usborne Quicklinks are updated. However, the content of a website may change at any time and Usborne Publishing is not responsible for the content on any website other than its own.

We recommend that children are supervised while on the Internet, that they do not use Internet chat rooms, and that you use Internet filtering software to block unsuitable material. Please ensure that your children read and follow the safety guidelines printed on the left.

For more information, see the "Net Help" area on the Usborne Quicklinks Website.

Computer not essential

If you don't have access to the Internet, don't worry. This book is a complete, self-contained reference book on its own.

Contents

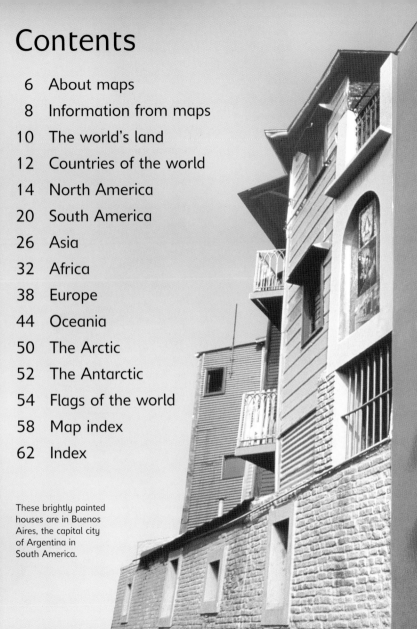

These brightly painted
houses are in Buenos
Aires, the capital city
of Argentina in
South America.

About maps

An atlas is a collection of maps. Maps are pictures of areas, seen from above. They show places much smaller than they really are. Some maps show the whole world, and some show much smaller areas, like cities or streets.

SOUTH AMERICA

What will you see on a map?

Maps should be easy to understand. Different kinds of shading and symbols help show what a place is like. A key explains what they all mean.

The size of a map compared with the real-life area it shows is called its scale. Some maps have a line called a scale bar that shows you the real distances between places on the map.

Key to South and Central America map
- Forest
- Desert
- Grassland
- Mountain
- Crops

This map shows what the land in South and Central America is like.

Scale bar ——
Scale
0km   2,000km
0 miles   1,240 miles

Which way is up?

The Earth doesn't really have a top and a bottom. Maps are often drawn with north at the top, though, to make them easier for everyone to understand.

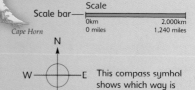

This compass symbol shows which way is north (N), south (S), east (E) and west (W).

Sea and land

More than two-thirds of the Earth is covered in salty water – the seas and oceans. Maps usually show water in blue.

The rest of the Earth is covered in land. Maps sometimes shade the land as it would look from above. Grasslands are often green and deserts can be sandy brown or yellow.

An island is land with water all around it. This is one of the Solomon Islands, in the Pacific Ocean.

Countries and continents

The land is divided into seven huge areas called continents, which are split into smaller areas called countries. Each country is run by a government and has its own laws. Some large countries are further divided into states, to make them easier to run.

Internet link

For a link to a website where you can play a memory game about continents, go to **www.usborne-quicklinks.com**

This is the continent of North America. It is a large area of land and islands.

North America is divided into countries, including Canada, the USA and Mexico.

The USA is divided into 50 different states. Each state can make its own laws.

Information from maps

Maps can show different things about the same area. Some maps show where countries and cities are. Some show what the land looks like or what kinds of plants grow there.

Political maps show countries and place names. The lines between countries are called borders or boundaries.

Physical maps show what the land looks like. They show features like mountains, lakes and rivers.

Thematic maps show other information, such as what the land is used for, or how many people live there.

Weather and wildlife

Different parts of the world have their own weather patterns, plants and wildlife. These areas are called biomes. Deserts, grasslands and rainforests are biomes. They can all be shown on a thematic map.

These cacti live in the desert, where it hardly ever rains. They store water in their stems.

Internet link

For a link to a website where you can find out more about biomes, go to **www.usborne-quicklinks.com**

How many people?

The people who live in an area are its population. Maps can be used to show which parts of an area are crowded, and which parts have very few people living in them.

This map of North America shows the areas where most people live.

Key
people in each
km² (0.39 sq miles)

- None
- Fewer than 1
- Up to 100
- More than 100

Towns and cities

Anywhere where a group of people live is called a settlement. A village is a small settlement, a town is bigger, and the largest kind is a city. The capital city of a country is where its government is based. About half the people in the world live in a town or a city.

Lines on maps

To make it easy to measure distances and find places on a map, the Earth is divided up with imaginary lines. The two sets of lines are called longitude and latitude. They are numbered in degrees (°) and minutes (′).

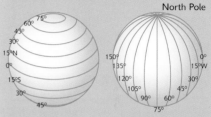

Lines of latitude run around the globe. On maps they usually run from left to right.

Longitude lines run from the North to the South Pole, and usually from top to bottom on maps.

This drawing of the Earth shows the North Pole and the main lines of longitude and latitude.

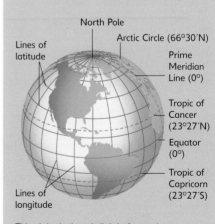

This globe is tipped slightly forward so the North Pole shows. This means that you can't quite see the South Pole.

The world's land

This is a physical map. It shows the different kinds of land in each continent.

The top half of the globe is called the northern hemisphere.

The bottom half of the globe is called the southern hemisphere.

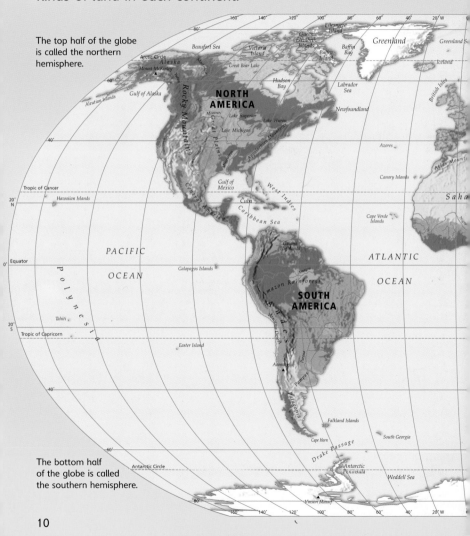

Ellesmere Island
Queen Elizabeth Islands
Greenland
Greenland S
Beaufort Sea
Victoria Island
Baffin Bay
Baffin Island
Iceland
Arctic Circle
Alaska
Great Bear Lake
British Isles
Mount McKinley
Hudson Bay
Labrador Sea
Gulf of Alaska
Rocky Mountains
NORTH AMERICA
Newfoundland
Aleutian Islands
Missouri
Lake Superior
Lake Huron
Great Plains
Lake Michigan
Appalachian Mountains
Azores
Atlas Mount
Tropic of Cancer
Hawaiian Islands
Gulf of Mexico
Canary Islands
Saha
Cuba
West Indies
Central America
Cape Verde Islands
Caribbean Sea
Niger
PACIFIC
Guiana Highlands
ATLANTIC
Equator
Galapagos Islands
Amazon Rainforest
OCEAN
OCEAN
Polynesia
SOUTH AMERICA
Andes
Tahiti
Madeira
Tropic of Capricorn
Easter Island
Parana
Aconcagua
Pampas
Falkland Islands
South Georgia
Cape Horn
Patagonia
Drake Passage
Antarctic Circle
Antarctic Peninsula
Weddell Sea
Vinson Massif

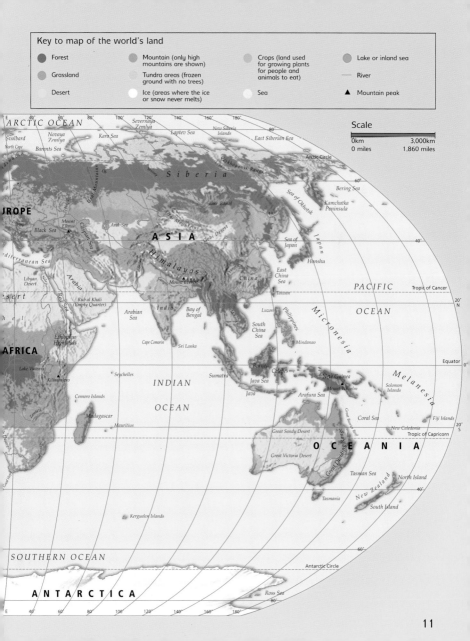

Key to map of the world's land

- **Forest**
- **Grassland**
- **Desert**
- **Mountain** (only high mountains are shown)
- **Tundra areas** (frozen ground with no trees)
- **Ice** (areas where the ice or snow never melts)
- **Crops** (land used for growing plants for people and animals to eat)
- **Sea**
- **Lake or inland sea**
- **River**
- ▲ **Mountain peak**

Scale

0km   3,000km
0 miles   1,860 miles

ARCTIC OCEAN

Svalbard
North Cape
Barents Sea
Novaya Zemlya
Severnaya Zemlya
Kara Sea
Laptev Sea
New Siberia Islands
East Siberian Sea
Arctic Circle

EUROPE

Ural Mountains
Ob
S i b e r i a
Verkhoyansk Range
Bering Sea
Kamchatka Peninsula
Sea of Okhotsk

Mount Elbrus
Black Sea
Caspian Sea
Aral Sea
Lake Baikal
Altai Mountains
A S I A
Gobi Desert
Sea of Japan
Japan
Honshu

Mediterranean Sea
Libyan Desert
Nile
Red Sea
Arabia
Rub al Khali (Empty Quarter)
H i m a l a y a s
Great Mount Everest ▲
China
East China Sea
Taiwan
PACIFIC
OCEAN
Tropic of Cancer
20° N

Sahel
Ethiopian Highlands
Arabian Sea
India
Bay of Bengal
Cape Comorin
Sri Lanka
Luzon
Philippines
Mindanao
South China Sea
M i c r o n e s i a

AFRICA
Lake Victoria
Kilimanjaro ▲
Seychelles
INDIAN
OCEAN
Sumatra
Borneo
Celebes
Java Sea
Java
New Guinea
Mount Wilhelm ▲
Melanesia
Solomon Islands
Equator
0°

Comoro Islands
Madagascar
Mauritius
Arafura Sea
Great Barrier Reef
Coral Sea
New Caledonia
Fiji Islands
Tropic of Capricorn
20° S

Zambezi
Great Sandy Desert
O C E A N I A

Desert
Great Victoria Desert
Great Dividing Range
Tasman Sea
New Zealand
North Island
40°

Kerguelen Islands
Tasmania
South Island

SOUTHERN OCEAN
Antarctic Circle
60°

A N T A R C T I C A
Ross Sea
80°

Countries of the world

This is a political map. It shows the different countries that make up each continent. Can you find your country on the map?

Scale

0km   3,000km
0 miles   1,860 miles

ARCTIC OCEAN

Svalbard (Norway)

RUSSIA

Arctic Circle

FINLAND
ESTONIA
LATVIA
LITHUANIA
BELARUS
POLAND
UKRAINE
CZECH REP
SLOVAKIA
HUNGARY
MOLDOVA
ROMANIA
BULGARIA
GREECE
TURKEY

KAZAKHSTAN

MONGOLIA

Caspian Sea
Black Sea
GEORGIA
ARM. AZER.
UZBEKISTAN
KYRGYZSTAN
TURKMENISTAN
TAJIKISTAN

CYPRUS
LEB.
SYRIA
IRAQ
ISRAEL
JORDAN
KUWAIT
AFGHANISTAN
PAKISTAN

IRAN

NORTH KOREA
SOUTH KOREA

JAPAN

PACIFIC OCEAN

Mediterranean Sea

LIBYA
EGYPT
SAUDI ARABIA
BAHRAIN
QATAR
U.A.E.
OMAN
YEMEN

NEPAL
BHUTAN
BANGLA-DESH
BURMA (MYANMAR)

CHINA

TAIWAN

Tropic of Cancer

INDIA

LAOS
THAILAND
VIETNAM
CAMBODIA

Northern Mariana Islands (U.S.A.)

20° N

CHAD
SUDAN

ERITREA
DJIBOUTI
ETHIOPIA
SOMALIA

CENTRAL AFRICAN REPUBLIC
CAMEROON

PHILIPPINES

MARSHALL ISLANDS

SRI LANKA

MALDIVES

MALAYSIA
BRUNEI
SINGAPORE

PALAU

FEDERATED STATES OF MICRONESIA

Equator
0°

CONGO (DEMOCRATIC REPUBLIC)
UGANDA
KENYA
RWANDA
BURUNDI
TANZANIA

SEYCHELLES

INDONESIA

EAST TIMOR

PAPUA NEW GUINEA

SOLOMON ISLANDS

NAURU
KIRIBATI

TUVALU

INDIAN OCEAN

COMOROS

ANGOLA
ZAMBIA
MALAWI
ZIMBABWE
MOZAMBIQUE
BOTSWANA
SWAZILAND
LESOTHO
SOUTH AFRICA
NAMIBIA

MADAGASCAR
MAURITIUS
Réunion (France)

Coral Sea Islands Territory (Australia)

VANUATU

New Caledonia (France)

SAMOA

FIJI TONGA

Tropic of Capricorn
20° S

AUSTRALIA

40°

Kerguelen Islands (France)

NEW ZEALAND

OCEAN

60°

Antarctic Circle

ANTARCTICA

80°

40°   60°   80°   100°   120°   140°   160°   180°

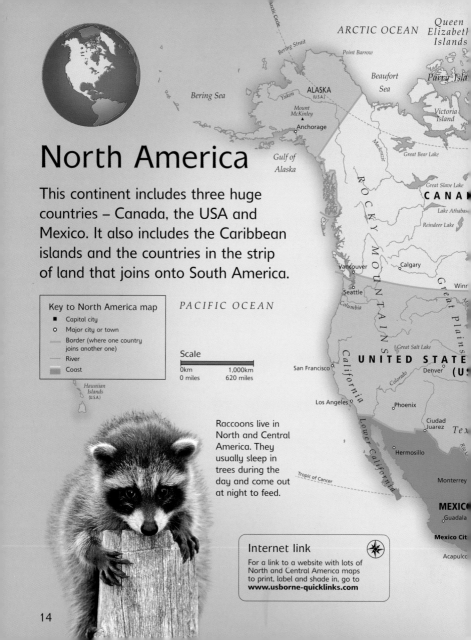

North America

This continent includes three huge countries – Canada, the USA and Mexico. It also includes the Caribbean islands and the countries in the strip of land that joins onto South America.

Key to North America map
- ■ Capital city
- ○ Major city or town
- — Border (where one country joins another one)
- — River
- ▬ Coast

Scale
0km   1,000km
0 miles   620 miles

Raccoons live in North and Central America. They usually sleep in trees during the day and come out at night to feed.

Internet link
For a link to a website with lots of North and Central America maps to print, label and shade in, go to **www.usborne-quicklinks.com**

ARCTIC OCEAN

Queen Elizabeth Islands

Parry Isla

Point Barrow

Beaufort Sea

ALASKA (U.S.A.)

Yukon

Mount McKinley ▲

Anchorage

Victoria Island

Bering Strait

Bering Sea

Gulf of Alaska

Mackenzie

Great Bear Lake

Great Slave Lake

CANA

Lake Athabas

Reindeer Lake

PACIFIC OCEAN

Vancouver

Seattle

Columbia

Calgary

Winr

Great Plains

R O C K Y   M O U N T A I N S

Great Salt Lake

UNITED STATE

San Francisco

Colorado

Denver

(U.

Los Angeles

California

Phoenix

Hawaiian Islands (U.S.A.)

Ciudad Juarez

Tex

Lower California

Hermosillo

Tropic of Cancer

Monterrey

MEXICO

Guadala

Mexico Cit

Acapulco

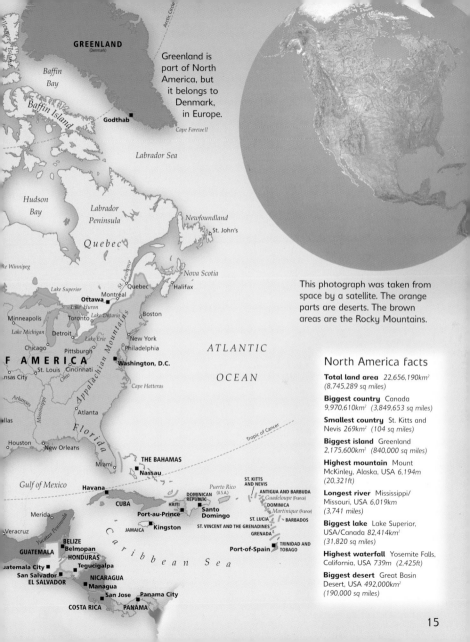

GREENLAND
(Denmark)

Greenland is part of North America, but it belongs to Denmark, in Europe.

Baffin Bay

Baffin Island

Godthab

Cape Farewell

Labrador Sea

Hudson Bay

Labrador Peninsula

Newfoundland

ke Winnipeg

Quebec

St. John's

Lake Superior

Minneapolis

Lake Huron

Montreal

Ottawa

Lake Ontario

Toronto

Detroit

Lake Michigan

Chicago

Pittsburgh

Lake Erie

Quebec

Nova Scotia

Halifax

Boston

New York

Philadelphia

ATLANTIC

OCEAN

This photograph was taken from space by a satellite. The orange parts are deserts. The brown areas are the Rocky Mountains.

F A M E R I C A

nsas City

St. Louis

Cincinnati

Washington, D.C.

Ohio

Arkansas

allas

Atlanta

Mississippi

Cape Hatteras

Florida

Houston

New Orleans

Appalachian Mountains

Miami

Gulf of Mexico

Havana

THE BAHAMAS

Nassau

Merida

CUBA

Puerto Rico (U.S.A.)

ST. KITTS AND NEVIS

ANTIGUA AND BARBUDA

Guadeloupe (France)

Veracruz

Yucatan Peninsula

JAMAICA

HAITI

DOMINICAN REPUBLIC

Port-au-Prince

Santo Domingo

Kingston

DOMINICA

Martinique (France)

ST. LUCIA

BARBADOS

ST. VINCENT AND THE GRENADINES

GRENADA

BELIZE

Belmopan

GUATEMALA

Guatemala City

San Salvador

EL SALVADOR

HONDURAS

Tegucigalpa

NICARAGUA

Managua

San Jose

Panama City

COSTA RICA

PANAMA

Port-of-Spain

TRINIDAD AND TOBAGO

C a r i b b e a n   S e a

Tropic of Cancer

North America facts

Total land area 22,656,190km² (8,745,289 sq miles)

Biggest country Canada 9,970,610km² (3,849,653 sq miles)

Smallest country St. Kitts and Nevis 269km² (104 sq miles)

Biggest island Greenland 2,175,600km² (840,000 sq miles)

Highest mountain Mount McKinley, Alaska, USA 6,194m (20,321ft)

Longest river Mississippi/ Missouri, USA 6,019km (3,741 miles)

Biggest lake Lake Superior, USA/Canada 82,414km² (31,820 sq miles)

Highest waterfall Yosemite Falls, California, USA 739m (2,425ft)

Biggest desert Great Basin Desert, USA 492,000km² (190,000 sq miles)

15

Using the land

Much of the land in North America is hard to live and work on. Some areas are hot and rocky, and some are freezing and snowy. In other parts of North America, the land and weather are just right for farming.

Shapes in the rock

In the southwest USA, some of the rocky land has slowly been worn away by rivers to make channels called canyons. Strong winds and rain have worn the rock away even more, making strange, rippling shapes.

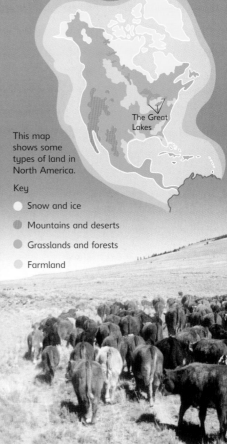

This map shows some types of land in North America.

The Great Lakes

Key

● Snow and ice

● Mountains and deserts

● Grasslands and forests

● Farmland

This strange photograph shows part of a small canyon in Arizona. The orange rock is called sandstone and the big cat is a puma.

Shaking ground

The Earth's crust is made up of huge slabs of rock, called plates. Sometimes they push or slide against each other, making the ground shake. This is called an earthquake. The San Andreas Fault, in the west of the USA, is a place where two plates slide past each other. Earthquakes often happen there.

This house fell down after a big earthquake in San Francisco, a city on the San Andreas Fault.

Massive farms

In the USA, Canada and Mexico, there are many huge cattle farms, called ranches. The cattle are farmed for their meat and skins. Other farms in North America grow crops such as corn and vegetables in enormous fields.

Internet link

For a link to a website with a clickable map and photographs of the biggest canyon in the world, go to **www.usborne-quicklinks.com**

One of the best ways for cowboys to move around their land and round up cattle is on horseback. Some farms are so big it would take days to walk across them.

Cities and celebrations

Explorers from Europe arrived in North America a few hundred years ago. But people have lived there for many thousands of years. Today, people come from all over the world to live there.

Stone cities

The Maya and the Aztec people lived in Mexico before European settlers came. The Maya built beautiful cities and pyramid-shaped temples out of stone. Ruins of these can still be seen today, on the Yucatan Peninsula in Mexico.

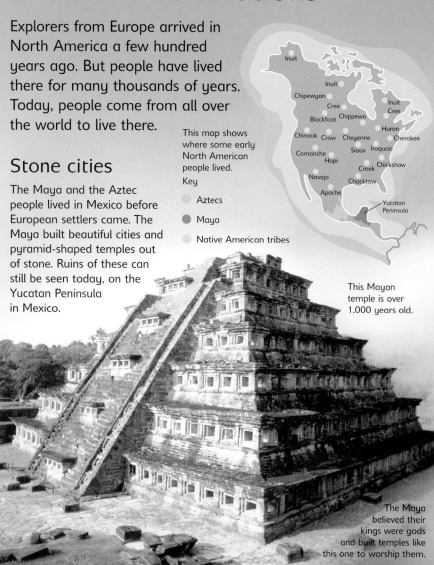

This map shows where some early North American people lived.

Key

- Aztecs
- Maya
- Native American tribes

Inuit
Inuit
Chipewyan
Cree
Inuit
Cree
Blackfoot
Chippewa
Chinook
Crow
Cheyenne
Huron
Comanche
Sioux
Iroquois
Cherokee
Hopi
Creek
Chickshaw
Navajo
Chocktaw
Apache
Yucatan Peninsula

This Mayan temple is over 1,000 years old.

The Maya believed their kings were gods and built temples like this one to worship them.

Busy city

New York City is the biggest city in the USA, and also one of the largest cities in the world. Almost 20 million people live there, and thousands more visit every year.

Internet link

For a link to a website where you can find lots more information about New York and see a slide show, go to **www.usborne-quicklinks.com**

Part of New York is on an island called Manhattan. Bridges join Manhattan to the rest of the city.

Icy homeland

Inuit people live in the icy north of Canada, in an area called Nunavut. It's too cold to grow crops there, so Inuit hunters catch animals and fish for people to eat.

This Inuit man is making a harpoon spear to take hunting. He is wearing warm fur clothes.

Calypso music

People visit the Caribbean islands for warm weather and sandy beaches. The islands are also famous for calypso music, which people play on drums made out of old oil cans.

This girl is dressed for Trinidad's carnival. Dancing and music are an important part of the celebrations.

South America

South America stretches down from the equator almost as far as the Antarctic. It is joined to North America by a narrow strip of land at the edge of Colombia.

Key to South America map

- ■ Capital city
- ○ Major city or town
- ― Border (where one country joins another one)
- ― River
- ▮ Coast

Scale

| 0km | 1,000km |
| 0 miles | 620 miles |

Caribbean Sea

Maracaibo · **Caracas**

VENEZUELA

Medellin · **Bogota**

Guiana Highlan

Cali · **COLOMBIA**

Orinoco

Equator

Quito

ECUADOR

Guayaquil

Galapagos Islands (Ecuador)

Negro

Amazon

Amazon Rainfores

PERU

Ucayali

Mad

Lima ·

ANDES

Lake Titicaca

BOLIVIA

La Paz

Sucre

Atacama Desert

Tropic of Capricorn

CHILE

PACIFIC

ANDES

San Migu de Tucum

OCEAN

Aconcagua ▲ Cordoba

Rosa

Santiago ·

ARGENTIN

Pamp

Patagonia

Strait of Magellan

Tierra del Fue

Cape Horn

Drake Passe

This is a toucan. Toucans live in South American rainforests. They use their long beaks to pick and eat fruit from the trees.

ATLANTIC
OCEAN

Georgetown
Paramaribo
Cayenne
ANA
URINAM   **FRENCH**
GUIANA
(France)

Equator

Amazon
Reservoir
us
Xingu
Tucurui Reservoir
Belem
Fortaleza

B R A Z I L

Tocantins
Sobradinho
Reservoir
Recife

Plateau of
Mato Grosso
São Francisco
Brazilian Highlands
Salvador

Brasilia
Goiania

Belo Horizonte

Parana
Furnas
Reservoir
Rio de Janeiro
São Paulo

Tropic of Capricorn

AGUAY
Asuncion
Curitiba

Porto Alegre

ATLANTIC
OCEAN

RUGUAY
Montevideo
enos Aires

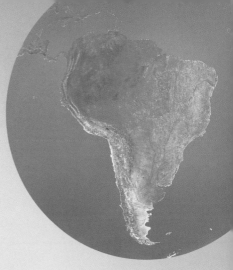

This is what South America looks like from space. The mottled strip along the west coast shows the Andes Mountains.

South America facts

Total land area *17,866,130km²*
(6,898,113 sq miles)

Biggest country Brazil *8,547,400km²*
(3,300,151 sq miles)

Smallest country Surinam *163,270km²*
(63,039 sq miles)

Biggest island Tierra del Fuego *46,360km²*
(17,900 sq miles)

Highest mountain Aconcagua, Argentina
6,959m (22,831ft)

Longest river Amazon, Brazil *6,440km*
(4,000 miles)

Biggest lake Lake Maracaibo, Venezuela
13,312km² (5,140 sq miles)

Highest waterfall Angel Falls,
on the Churun River, Venezuela
979m (3,212ft)

Biggest desert Patagonian Desert,
Argentina *673,000km²*
(260,000 sq miles)

Internet link

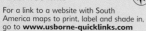

and Islands
(U.K.)

For a link to a website with South America maps to print, label and shade in, go to **www.usborne-quicklinks.com**

21

Wettest and driest

South America has one of the wettest places on Earth in it – the Amazon Rainforest. But it also has the Atacama Desert, which is one of the driest. South America's Andes Mountains make up the the longest chain of mountains in the world.

Snowy peaks

The Andes Mountains are over 7,000km (4,300 miles) long, and stretch all the way down the continent. The lower slopes are good for farming, but the high peaks are snowy and bleak. More than 30 of the peaks in the Andes are volcanoes.

This map shows some of the landscape features of South America.

This climber is close to the top of Huascaran, one of the highest peaks in the Andes.

Key

● Amazon Rainforest

⋎ Rivers in the Amazon

○ Atacama Desert

Andes Mountains

Forest homes

The Amazon Rainforest is the biggest rainforest in the world. It's always hot there and it rains nearly every day. The forest is home to a huge number of plants and animals.

This blue morpho butterfly comes from the Amazon. It's as big as a man's hand.

Internet link

For a link to a website where you can take a walk through a rainforest, meeting animals along the way, go to **www.usborne-quicklinks.com**

Mighty river

There's more water in the Amazon River than in any other river in the world. Over 1,000 smaller rivers flow into it, from all over the north part of South America. It is also one of the longest rivers, and winds nearly all the way across the top of the continent.

This boy is paddling his boat along the Amazon River. The main part of the river is so wide there are no bridges over it.

Dry ground

The Atacama Desert, in Chile, is next to the Pacific Ocean but it is the driest place on the planet. In some parts of the desert, people think it may never have rained at all.

Desert plants like these have long roots to reach way down into the cracked earth for water.

Places for living

South Americans live high in the mountains, deep in the rainforest, and even in the desert. Many people live in tiny farming villages, but South America also has some of the biggest cities in the world.

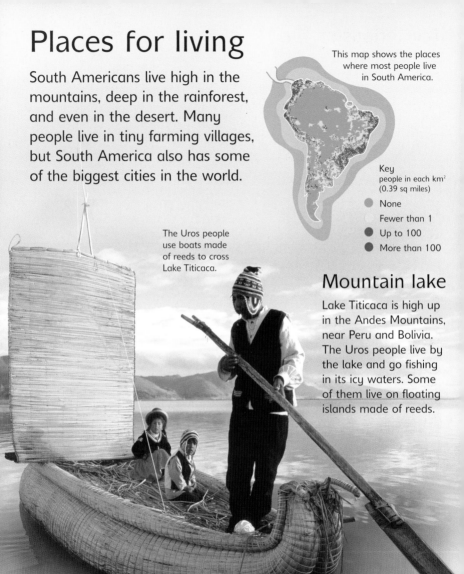

This map shows the places where most people live in South America.

Key
people in each km²
(0.39 sq miles)

- None
- Fewer than 1
- Up to 100
- More than 100

The Uros people use boats made of reeds to cross Lake Titicaca.

Mountain lake

Lake Titicaca is high up in the Andes Mountains, near Peru and Bolivia. The Uros people live by the lake and go fishing in its icy waters. Some of them live on floating islands made of reeds.

Mysterious statues

Easter Island, in the Pacific Ocean, is covered in hundreds of stone figures called *moai*. They were made by the first people who lived there, to worship their ancestors.

Most *moai* statues are at least twice the height of a man, and very heavy. How they were moved into place is a mystery.

City celebration

Early every year, the busy city of Rio de Janeiro in Brazil holds a carnival. It lasts for five days, with feasting, music and costume parades. Dancers take part in samba competitions across the city.

At carnival time in Rio de Janeiro, floats like this one carry costumed people through the streets of the city.

Internet link

For a link to a website with pictures of Andean people and songs to listen to, go to **www.usborne-quicklinks.com**

Asia

Asia is the biggest
continent. It stretches
from the Arctic Circle to
the equator, and from
the Ural Mountains in
the west to the Pacific
Ocean in the east.

The part
of Russia on
this side of
the Ural
Mountains
is in Europe.

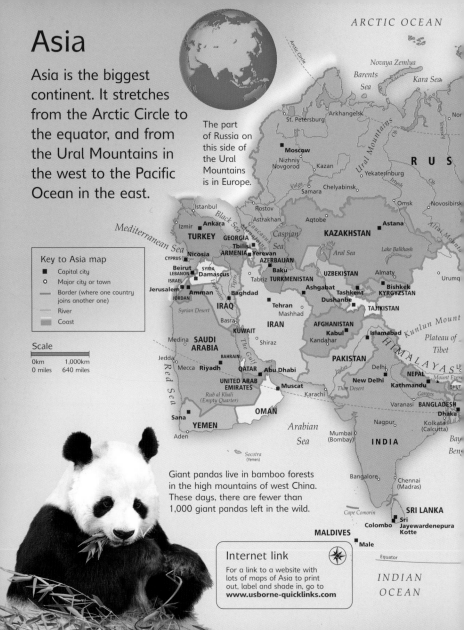

ARCTIC OCEAN

Novaya Zemlya
Barents
Sea
Kara Sea
Arctic Circle

St. Petersburg   Arkhangelsk
Moscow
Nizhniy
Novgorod   Kazan
Volga   Samara   Chelyabinsk
Yekaterinburg
Omsk   Novosibirsk

R U S

Ural Mountains   Ob
Irtysh

Istanbul   Rostov
Izmir   Ankara   Astrakhan   Aqtobe
TURKEY   GEORGIA   Caspian   KAZAKHSTAN   Astana
Mediterranean Sea   Black Sea   Tbilisi   Sea   Aral Sea   Lake Balkhash   Altai Mountains
Nicosia   ARMENIA Yerevan   Almaty
CYPRUS   AZERBAIJAN   UZBEKISTAN   Urumqi
Beirut   Baku   Bishkek   KYRGYZSTAN
LEBANON   SYRIA   Damascus   Tabriz   TURKMENISTAN   Tashkent
ISRAEL   Ashgabat   Dushanbe
Jerusalem   Amman   Baghdad   Tehran   TAJIKISTAN
JORDAN   Mashhad   Kunlun Mount
IRAQ   AFGHANISTAN   Plateau of
Basra   IRAN   Kabul   Islamabad   Tibet
KUWAIT   Kandahar   HIMALAYAS   Mount Evere
Medina   Shiraz   PAKISTAN   Delhi   NEPAL   BHUT
SAUDI   BAHRAIN   New Delhi   Kathmandu
Jedda   ARABIA   QATAR   Abu Dhabi   Indus   Ganges
Mecca   Riyadh   UNITED ARAB   Muscat   Thar Desert   Varanasi   BANGLADESH
EMIRATES   Karachi   Dhaka
Rub al Khali   OMAN   Nagpur   Kolkata
(Empty Quarter)   (Calcutta)
Sana   YEMEN   Arabian   Mumbai   INDIA   Bay
Aden   Sea   (Bombay)   Beng
Socotra
(Yemen)
Bangalore   Chennai
(Madras)
SRI LANKA
Cape Comorin   Sri
Colombo   Jayewardenepura
MALDIVES   Kotte
Male
Equator
INDIAN
OCEAN

Syrian Desert
Euphrates
Tigris

Red Sea
The Gulf

Key to Asia map
- ■ Capital city
- ○ Major city or town
- — Border (where one country
  joins another one)
- — River
- ▨ Coast

Scale
0km   1,000km
0 miles   640 miles

Giant pandas live in bamboo forests
in the high mountains of west China.
These days, there are fewer than
1,000 giant pandas left in the wild.

Internet link

For a link to a website with
lots of maps of Asia to print
out, label and shade in, go to
www.usborne-quicklinks.com

The white ridges across the middle of this satellite photograph of Asia are the snowy mountaintops of the Himalayas.

Asia facts

Total land area
44,537,920km²
(17,196,090 sq miles)

Biggest country Russia
Total area: 17,075,200km²
(6,592,735 sq miles) Asiatic Russia:
12,780,800km² (4,934,667 sq miles)

Smallest country Maldives
300km² (116 sq miles)

Biggest island Borneo
751,100km² (290,000 sq miles)

Highest mountain Mount
Everest, Nepal/China *8,850m*
(29,035ft)

Longest river Yangtze
(Chang Jiang), China *6,380km*
(3,964 miles)

Biggest lake Caspian Sea,
western Asia *370,999km²*
(143,243 sq miles)

Highest waterfall Jog Falls, India
253m (830ft)

Biggest desert Arabian Desert
(deserts of Saudi Arabia)
2,230,000km² (900,000 sq miles)

All kinds of land

Asia has almost every kind of landscape you can think of. In the north, there are freezing forests. To the south, there are deserts and rainforests. Much of central Asia is covered in grassland.

Rice terraces

Some parts of Asia are very hilly. Farmers there make flat shelves called terraces in the land, to grow their crops on. The terraces stop water from running away down the slope, so the rice can grow. Many Asian farmers grow rice in this way.

These hillside terraces make flat areas for rice crops to grow.

High mountains

The highest mountains in the world are the Himalayas. They run through India, Nepal, Bhutan and China. The tallest peak is Mount Everest. Each year, many climbers try to reach the top.

This photograph shows the top, or summit, of Mount Everest. Strong winds are blowing snow off the top.

Rainy seasons

India has two main seasons. One is very rainy, and the other is very dry. These changing seasons are caused by the way the wind blows, and are called monsoons. The monsoons affect when crops can grow.

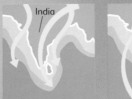

In winter, monsoon winds blow from the land out to sea. This is the dry season.

In summer, monsoon winds blow in from the sea, bringing rain. This is the wet season.

Great Wall of China

The people of China built an amazing wall hundreds of years ago, to protect their country from enemies. The Great Wall of China passes through deserts, mountains and grasslands along the northern edge of China. It is so long, it can be seen from space.

Internet link

For a link to a website where you can take a quiz and reach the top of Mount Everest, go to **www.usborne-quicklinks.com**

The Great Wall of China is made of stone. These watch-towers helped soldiers see their enemies coming.

Many ways of life

Some areas of Asia have hardly any people living in them, but others are very crowded. People across Asia have lots of different beliefs and customs. Ancient traditions often survive alongside modern ways of life.

Tallest buildings

Among the tallest buildings in the world are the Petronas Towers in Kuala Lumpur, the capital city of Malaysia. They are 452m (1,438ft) high, and have 88 floors, which are used for offices.

This market trader is taking fresh vegetables to sell at the floating market near Bangkok, in Thailand.

The Petronas Towers are much taller than other skyscrapers nearby.

Floating market

Every morning, small boats filled with fruit and vegetables form a floating market on a stretch of canal, near Bangkok in Thailand. Market traders paddle along the canal, selling food and souvenirs to local people and tourists.

Crowded country

China has the biggest population of any country. Over one-fifth of all the people in the world live there. Most of them live in big cities, though. In some parts of China, there are no people at all.

Internet link

For a link to a website where you can see slide shows and read about Asian countries, go to **www.usborne-quicklinks.com**

Key
people in each km²
(0.39 sq miles)

- None (deserts)
- Fewer than 1
- Up to 100
- More than 100

This map shows where most people live in China.

Glittering spires

Many of the world's religions started in Asia. Buddhism began in India and spread to other Asian countries, including Burma. There are many Buddhist temples in Burma. They are often decorated with pointed spires and large gold statues.

These golden spires are part of a Buddhist temple in Mandalay, Burma.

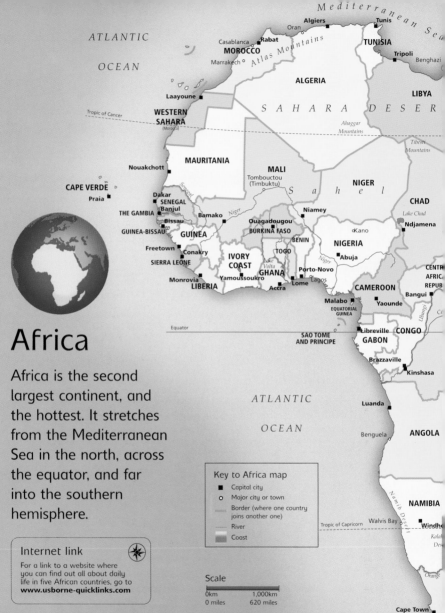

ATLANTIC

OCEAN

Mediterranean Sea

Oran Algiers Tunis

Casablanca Rabat TUNISIA

MOROCCO Tripoli Benghazi

Marrakech Atlas Mountains

ALGERIA LIBYA

Laayoune

Tropic of Cancer

WESTERN S A H A R A   D E S E R

SAHARA

(Morocco) *Ahaggar Mountains* *Tibesti Mountains*

MAURITANIA MALI

Nouakchott Tombouctou NIGER CHAD

(Timbuktu) *Lake Chad*

CAPE VERDE *S a h e l* Ndjamena

Praia Niamey oKano

Dakar SENEGAL Bamako

THE GAMBIA Banjul Niger Ouagadougou NIGERIA

Bissau BURKINA FASO Abuja

GUINEA-BISSAU GUINEA BENIN

Freetown Conakry TOGO Niger

SIERRA LEONE IVORY Lake Porto-Novo

COAST Volta GHANA Lagos CENTRAL

Monrovia Yamoussoukro Lome CAMEROON AFRIC

LIBERIA Accra Malabo Yaounde REPUB

EQUATORIAL Bangui

GUINEA

Equator Libreville CONGO

SAO TOME GABON

AND PRINCIPE Brazzaville

Kinshasa

ATLANTIC

Luanda

OCEAN ANGOLA

Benguela

Key to Africa map

■ Capital city

○ Major city or town *Namib Desert*

Border (where one country Tropic of Capricorn Walvis Bay NAMIBIA

joins another one) Windh

River *Kalah*

Coast Cape Town

Cape of Good Hope

Africa

Africa is the second
largest continent, and
the hottest. It stretches
from the Mediterranean
Sea in the north, across
the equator, and far
into the southern
hemisphere.

Internet link

For a link to a website where
you can find out all about daily
life in five African countries, go to
www.usborne-quicklinks.com

Scale

0km   1,000km
0 miles   620 miles

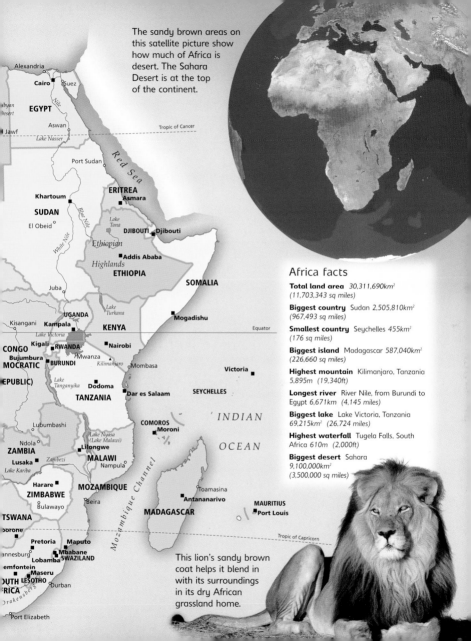

The sandy brown areas on this satellite picture show how much of Africa is desert. The Sahara Desert is at the top of the continent.

Map labels

Alexandria
Cairo — Suez
EGYPT
Libyan Desert
Nile
Jawf
Aswan
Lake Nasser
Tropic of Cancer
Port Sudan
Red Sea
Khartoum
SUDAN
ERITREA
Asmara
El Obeid
Blue Nile
White Nile
Lake Tana
DJIBOUTI — Djibouti
Ethiopian Highlands
Addis Ababa
ETHIOPIA
Juba
SOMALIA
Lake Turkana
Kisangani
UGANDA
Kampala
Mogadishu
Equator
CONGO (DEMOCRATIC REPUBLIC)
Kigali
RWANDA
KENYA
Nairobi
Bujumbura
BURUNDI
Mwanza
Lake Victoria
Kilimanjaro
Mombasa
Lubumbashi
Lake Tanganyika
Dodoma
Dar es Salaam
TANZANIA
Victoria
SEYCHELLES
Ndola
Lake Nyasa (Lake Malawi)
COMOROS
Moroni
INDIAN OCEAN
ZAMBIA
Lusaka
Zambezi
Lilongwe
MALAWI
Nampula
Lake Kariba
Harare
ZIMBABWE
MOZAMBIQUE
Bulawayo
Beira
Mozambique Channel
Toamasina
Antananarivo
MAURITIUS
Port Louis
MADAGASCAR
BOTSWANA
Gaborone
Pretoria — Maputo
Johannesburg
Lobamba
Mbabane
SWAZILAND
Bloemfontein
Maseru
SOUTH LESOTHO
AFRICA
Durban
Drakensberg
Port Elizabeth
Tropic of Capricorn

Africa facts

Total land area 30,311,690km² (11,703,343 sq miles)

Biggest country Sudan 2,505,810km² (967,493 sq miles)

Smallest country Seychelles 455km² (176 sq miles)

Biggest island Madagascar 587,040km² (226,660 sq miles)

Highest mountain Kilimanjaro, Tanzania 5,895m (19,340ft)

Longest river River Nile, from Burundi to Egypt 6,671km (4,145 miles)

Biggest lake Lake Victoria, Tanzania 69,215km² (26,724 miles)

Highest waterfall Tugela Falls, South Africa 610m (2,000ft)

Biggest desert Sahara 9,100,000km² (3,500,000 sq miles)

This lion's sandy brown coat helps it blend in with its surroundings in its dry African grassland home.

Vast desert

A large part of Africa is covered by the Sahara, the biggest desert in the world. It's very hot there during the day, but at night the temperature often drops below freezing.

Dry desert

Hardly any rain falls in the Sahara Desert. The driest part is in Libya, where the desert is sandy. The wind blows the sand into huge piles called dunes, that form dramatic, curving shapes.

This map shows the different kinds of landscapes in Africa.

Sahara Desert

Key

● Highlands
● Scrub
○ Desert
● Rainforest
● Savannah grasslands

Internet link

For a link to a website where you can discover more about the wildlife and people who live in the Sahara Desert, go to **www.usborne-quicklinks.com**

One of the best ways to cross the Sahara Desert is by camel. Camels can go a long time without water.

34

Thick rainforest

Some places in Africa have plenty of rain. The island of Madagascar is covered in thick, green rainforest. Many unusual animals, such as small, furry lemurs, live there.

Grassy plains

Large parts of Africa are hot grasslands called savannah. It's too dry there for many trees to grow, but there is enough rain for grasses. Savannah animals include lions, giraffes, elephants and zebras.

Ring-tailed lemurs live in the rainforests of Madagascar.

These zebras live in the savannah grasslands. The distant mountain is Kilimanjaro.

Farms and cities

Many people in Africa live in villages and work on farms. But now more and more people are moving to big cities to work and live.

This map shows the farming areas of Africa.

This is the Sahara Desert. No crops can grow here.

Thick rainforest

Key

● Farmland for crops and animals
○ Land not used for farming

Not enough water

Many parts of Africa don't get much rain. When there is too little rain, crops can't grow and people don't have enough water. This is called a drought. Sometimes, water may be carried or brought in pipes to a village where there is a drought.

This Zulu woman is carrying water in a clay pot.

Internet link

For a link to a website where you can find pictures and stories about life in Africa, as well as some fun things to do, go to **www.usborne-quicklinks.com**

Farming for money

There are farms in most parts of Africa. Some grow grains such as corn or millet for people living nearby to eat. Others grow crops such as coffee or cocoa, to sell to other countries.

Selling crops is a good way for a country to make money. But it may mean that the people can't grow enough food to eat themselves.

This man is picking tea in Burundi. The dried leaves will be sold to countries far away.

Growing city

Cape Town is one of the three capital cities of South Africa. It is built on flat land, close to the Atlantic Ocean, around the base of Table Mountain. Cape Town is a growing city. More and more people are moving there from the countryside to find better places to live and work.

This is Cape Town, in South Africa. The nearby mountain is covered in cloud.

37

Europe

Europe is a small continent, but it has many countries in it. Only the part of Russia west of the Ural Mountains is in Europe – the rest is in Asia.

Europe is home to many types of birds, such as this common European kingfisher.

ARCTIC OCEAN

Arctic Circle

Reykjavik
ICELAND

Norwegian Sea

SWEDEN

Bergen
NORWAY
Oslo

Stockholm
Lake Vaner

Gothenburg

British Isles

Edinburgh

Belfast

IRELAND
Dublin

UNITED KINGDOM

North Sea

DENMARK
Copenhagen

Baltic S

Gdans

Cardiff

London

Hamburg

ATLANTIC

OCEAN

English Channel

Amsterdam
NETHERLANDS
The Hague
Brussels
BELGIUM

Berlin

POLAN

Rhine

GERMANY

Elbe

Oder

LUXEMBOURG
Luxembourg

Prague

CZECH REPUBLIC

Nantes

Paris

Danube

Munich

Vienna

Bratis

Loire

FRANCE

Bern
SWITZERLAND
LIECHTENSTEIN
Vaduz

AUSTRIA

Budape

Bay of Biscay

Bordeaux

Lyon

The Alps

Milan

Turin

SLOVENIA
Ljubljana

Po

CROATIA
Zagreb

BOSNIA AND HERZEGOVIN
Sarajevo

Adriatic Sea

Bilbao

Oporto

ANDORRA
Andorra la Vella

MONACO
Marseille

SAN MARINO

ITALY

PORTUGAL

Madrid

Barcelona

Corsica (France)

Rome
VATICAN CITY

ALE
Ti

Lisbon

Tagus

SPAIN

Valencia

Naples

Cordoba

Sardinia (Italy)

Gibraltar *(U.K.)*

Mediterranean

Sicily (Italy)

MALTA Valletta

Sea

Key to Europe map

- ■ Capital city
- ○ Major city or town
- Border (where one country joins another one)
- River
- Coast

Scale

0km   500km
0 miles   310 miles

North Cape

Barents Sea

Murmansk

Kola
Peninsula

Arctic Circle

Ural Mountains

Pechora

The rest
of Russia
is in Asia.

apland

Oulu

FINLAND

Ukhta

Arkhangelsk

Northern Dvina

Lake Onega

R U S S I A

Perm

Lake Ladoga

elsinki

Helsinki

St. Petersburg

Cherepovets

Tallinn

ESTONIA

Rybinsk
Reservoir

Volga

Kama

Riga

LATVIA

Nizhniy Novgorod

Kazan

LITHUANIA

Vilnius

Moscow

Samara

SSIA

Minsk

Tula

BELARUS

Don

Volga

arsaw

Vistula

Voronezh

kow

Lviv

Kiev

Dnieper

Kharkiv

Volgograd

UKRAINE

Donetsk

Don

Volga

OVAKIA

Dnipropetrovsk

Astrakhan

Carpathian Mountains

Rostov

NGARY

MOLDOVA

Caspian
Sea

Cluj-Napoca

Chisinau

Odesa

Sea of
Azov

ROMANIA

Crimean
Peninsula

Caucasus Mountains

elgrade

Bucharest

Mount Elbrus

Danube

Black Sea

BIA AND
TENEGRO

BULGARIA

Sofia

Skopje

ACEDONIA

REECE

Aegean
Sea

Athens

Crete
(Greece)

Europe facts

Total land area 10,205,720km²
(3,940,428 sq miles)

Biggest country Russia
Total area: 17,075,200km²
(6,492,735 sq miles)
Area of European Russia:
4,294,400km² (658,068 sq miles)

Smallest country Vatican City
0.44km² (0.17 sq miles)

Biggest island Great Britain
229,870km² (90,506 sq miles)

Highest mountain Mount Elbrus,
Russia 5,642m (18,510ft)

Longest river Volga 3,700km
(2,298 miles)

Biggest lake Lake Ladoga, Russia
17,700km² (6,834 sq miles)

Highest waterfall Utigard, on
the Jostedal Glacier, Norway
800m (2,625ft)

Biggest desert There are no
deserts in Europe.

Internet link

For a link to a website where you
can explore a virtual castle, like one
you might find in Europe, go to
www.usborne-quicklinks.com

This satellite photograph
shows how Europe joins
onto Asia. The big, white
patch at the top is the ice
that covers the Arctic.

Farms and hills

A lot of the land in Europe is gently hilly and good for farming. Some areas are rocky or snowy, and fewer crops grow there.

This map shows some of the crops that grow in Europe.

Key

- ● Grapes
- ● Olives (for oil)
- ● Fruit
- ● Potatoes
- ● Grains, such as wheat and barley

Europe

Asia

Mediterranean Sea

Fruit and vegetables

The south of Europe is on the coast of the Mediterranean Sea. The weather there is very hot and dry in summer, but cool and wet in winter. Oranges, lemons and other citrus fruits grow well there, as well as many other kinds of fruit and vegetables.

This market is in Rome, in Italy. Every day, people bring fresh fruit and vegetables from the farms nearby, to sell at the market.

40

Natural hot water

The island of Iceland has natural hot water, heated by rocks under the Earth. From time to time, jets of steam and hot water burst out through holes in the ground. These jets are called geysers.

This is Strokkur Geyser, in Iceland. Boiling hot water erupts from it every few minutes.

Jagged peaks

The largest group of mountains in Europe is the Alps. They formed millions of years ago, out of giant folds of rock. They have very jagged shapes, which were carved out by rivers of ice, called glaciers.

This picture shows how some of the valleys and lower slopes of the Alps are used for farming crops. Behind, you can see much higher, snowy peaks.

Internet link

For a link to a website where you can visit European countries and see slide shows, go to **www.usborne-quicklinks.com**

Places to see

Europe is famous for its beautiful old cities and historic buildings. But many exciting modern buildings attract visitors too.

Eiffel Tower

The Eiffel Tower was built in 1889, in Paris, the capital city of France. Until 1930, it was the tallest tower in the world. Since it was built, more than 200 million people have visited it.

The Eiffel Tower in France is as tall as over 100 trucks stacked on top of each other.

Great cathedrals

Many cities in Europe have huge churches called cathedrals. They are made of carved stone, and took many years to build. Some have pointed spires on top, others have towers or rounded domes.

This is Cologne Cathedral in Germany. It took 600 years to build.

Modern buildings

There are some amazing modern buildings in Europe. One of the most interesting is Spain's Museo Guggenheim Bilbao. It is covered with huge curving sheets of metal.

This is the Museo Guggenheim Bilbao in Spain. It is a gallery where people go to look at modern art.

Roman remains

About 2,000 years ago, Rome was one of the biggest cities in the world. At that time, the Romans ruled all the lands around the Mediterranean Sea. Ruins of Roman buildings can still be seen in lots of places in Europe.

Internet link

For a link to a website where you can find out more about the Eiffel Tower and crazy tower stunts, go to **www.usborne-quicklinks.com**

This map shows where the Romans ruled in Europe. These lands were called the Roman Empire.

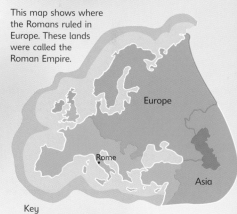

Europe

Rome

Asia

Key

● The Roman Empire

These are the remains of the Colosseum in Rome. People came here to see fighters called gladiators.

Oceania

Oceania is the smallest continent. It is made up of Australia, New Zealand and Papua New Guinea, as well as many smaller islands dotted across the Pacific Ocean.

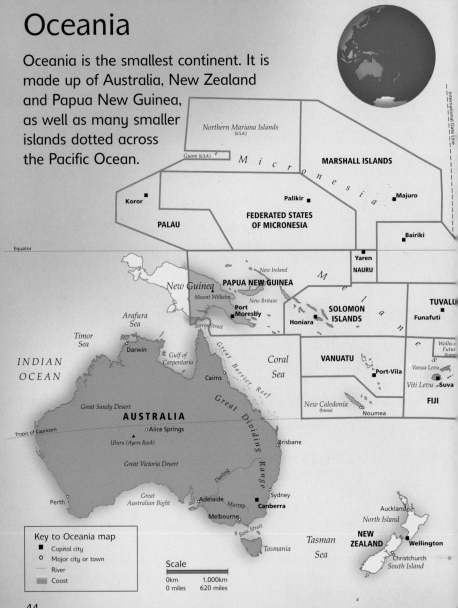

International Date Line

Northern Mariana Islands (U.S.A.)

Guam (U.S.A.)

M i c r o n e s i a

MARSHALL ISLANDS

Koror ■

Palikir ■

Majuro ■

PALAU

FEDERATED STATES OF MICRONESIA

Bairiki ■

Equator

Yaren ■
NAURU

New Ireland

PAPUA NEW GUINEA

M e l

New Guinea

▲ *Mount Wilhelm*

New Britain

Port Moresby ■

Torres Strait

Honiara ■

SOLOMON ISLANDS

a n e

TUVALU

Funafuti ■

s

Wallis e Futur France

Arafura Sea

Darwin ○

Gulf of Carpentaria

Cairns ○

Timor Sea

INDIAN OCEAN

Great Sandy Desert

AUSTRALIA

Alice Springs ○
▲ *Uluru (Ayers Rock)*

Great Victoria Desert

Great Barrier Reef

Great Dividing Range

Coral Sea

VANUATU

Port-Vila ■

Vanua Levu

Viti Levu Suva ■

FIJI

New Caledonia (France)

Noumea ○

Tropic of Capricorn

Darling

Brisbane ○

Perth ○

Great Australian Bight

Adelaide ○

Murray

Canberra ■

Sydney ○

Melbourne ○

Bass Strait

Tasmania

Tasman Sea

Auckland ○
North Island

NEW ZEALAND

Wellington ■

Christchurch ○
South Island

Key to Oceania map

■ Capital city
○ Major city or town
— River
▨ Coast

Scale

0km   1,000km
0 miles   620 miles

44

Oceania facts

Total land area 8,564,400km²
(3,306,715 sq miles)

Biggest country Australia 7,741,220km²
(2,988,885 sq miles)

Smallest country Nauru 21km² (8 sq miles)

Biggest island New Guinea 800,000km²
(309,000 sq miles)

Highest mountain Mount Wilhelm,
Papua New Guinea 4,509m (14,793ft)

Longest river Murray/Darling River Australia 3,718km
(2,310 miles)

Biggest lake Lake Eyre, Australia 9,000km²
(3,470 sq miles)

Highest waterfall Sutherland Falls on the Arthur
River, New Zealand 580m (1,904ft)

Biggest desert Great Victoria Desert, Australia
388,500km² (150,000 sq miles)

P o l y n e s i a

Equator   PACIFIC
OCEAN

KIRIBATI

Tokelau
(New Zealand)

AMOA
Apia

*American
Samoa*
(U.S.A.)

GA

Cook Islands
(New Zealand)

Niue
(New
Zealand)

alofa

Tahiti   *French Polynesia*
(France)

Tropic of Capricorn

International Date Line

Some of the countries in
Oceania are made up of hundreds
of islands, which are too small to
be seen on this map. The red lines
show where one country ends and
another begins.

*Pitcairn
Islands*
(U.K.)

This photograph was taken from
space. The light brown areas
show that much of Australia is
desert. The large, white area
below Australia is Antarctica.

Internet link

For a link to a website where
you can take a trip to Australia
and see a slide show, go to
www.usborne-quicklinks.com

Wallabies live
in the dry, dusty
grasslands of
Australia. Their long
eyelashes protect
their eyes from
blowing sand.

Desert and ocean

Oceania is made up of over 20,000 islands
in the Pacific Ocean. Most of them are tiny,
but the desert land of Australia is huge.
Many small islands are the tops
of underwater volcanoes.

The deepest place

The bottom of the Pacific Ocean is
covered in mountains, and valleys called
trenches. The deepest place on Earth is
in the Mariana Trench. It is over 11km
(6.8 miles) deep. If you dropped a small
rock into the sea, it would take over
an hour to reach the bottom of
the Mariana Trench.

These maps show the Mariana
Trench and the Challenger
Deep, which is its deepest part.

Japan
(Asia)

Philippines
(Asia)

Mariana
Islands

Mariana
Islands
(enlarged)

Guam

Key

● Islands

● Trench

● Challenger Deep

Ancient land

Most of Australia is a bare, rocky desert.
Its land has hardly changed for millions
of years. The rocks have slowly been
worn into smooth shapes by the
wind and rain.

Wave Rock in Australia looks
like a towering wall of water.
It was worn into this
unusual shape by
the wind and
rain.

Internet link
For a link to a website where you can
explore a coral reef and its creatures,
go to **www.usborne-quicklinks.com**

How islands form

The oldest islands in Oceania are made of limestone rock. The youngest islands are the tips of underwater volcanoes. These pictures show how an island forms and changes.

A volcano grows under the sea and rises up above the surface. When it stops erupting, animals and plants live on it.

Sea animals called corals grow around the edge of the dead volcano. They form a ring of coral called an atoll.

The coral dies and forms hard limestone. Forests grow on these new islands. The soft rock of the volcano is slowly worn away by the sea.

The middle part of this island in French Polynesia is a volcano. It is surrounded by coral reefs, which are large areas of tiny sea animals called corals.

Forests by the sea

Mangrove trees live on the edge of warm seas, with their roots partly underwater. Unlike most plants, they aren't harmed by salty sea water. Thick mangrove forests grow in Papua New Guinea and other islands in Oceania.

The roots of mangrove trees spread out wide and prop the trees up in the swampy ground.

Ocean living

Fewer people live in Oceania than on any other continent apart from Antarctica. Most of Oceania's people live near the sea.

Australia's people

Four out of five Australians live in towns and cities that are within one hour's drive of the sea. The rest live scattered across the huge desert area called the outback. People there live so far apart that some children have to do their schoolwork by mail or over the Internet.

Most Australians live near the sea, and many enjoy water sports. This man has found a good wave to surf, near a beach in Australia.

Original people

Most people in Australia and New Zealand today are related to people who came from Europe. But the first people in Australia were the Aboriginal people, thousands of years before. The first settlers in New Zealand were the Maoris.

This map shows how many people live in different parts of Australia.

Key
people in each
km² (0.39 sq miles)

● More than 50

● 4–50

2–4

1 – 2

Fewer than 1

These men are wearing traditional Maori costumes. All children in New Zealand learn about Maori traditions at school.

Internet link

For a link to a website with a selection of photographs from Papua New Guinea, go to **www.usborne-quicklinks.com**

Fiji's farmers

Many Fijians are farmers. They grow enough food, such as corn and vegetables, for their families and other people in their villages. Some of their crops, such as coconuts and sugar cane, are sold to other countries.

Farming people on Fiji often live in one-room houses like these, with thatched roofs and woven floor mats inside.

Dressing up

The Huli people live in the mountains of Papua New Guinea. Huli men paint their faces and dress in spectacular feathered wigs to perform dances, which are famous all over the world.

This Huli man is putting on face paint. His wig is made from grasses, and feathers from a bird called a cassowary.

The Arctic

The area around the North Pole is called the Arctic. There's no land at the North Pole, but the sea there is so cold that its surface freezes and turns to thick ice.

The white patch on this globe shows the parts of the Arctic that are always covered with ice.

Frozen land

The Arctic Circle is an imaginary line around the Arctic. Eight countries have land inside the Arctic Circle. This land is called tundra. The soil there is frozen for most of the year. No trees can grow, but lichen and moss plants grow close to the ground.

Coping with cold

Arctic animals have to survive freezing temperatures. Many have thick, bushy white coats to keep them warm and help them blend in with the snow. Some have a layer of fat for extra warmth.

This baby harp seal has thick fur, and a layer of fat under its skin to keep it warm.

Internet link

For a link to a website where you can take part in a quiz about animals that live in the Arctic, go to
www.usborne-quicklinks.com

Scale

0km   1,000km
0 miles   620 miles

PACIFIC

OCEAN

JAPAN

○ Sapporo

○ Petropavlosk-
Kamchatskiy

*Bering
Sea*

Aleutian Islands

○ Anadyr

Arctic Circle

RUSSIA

○ Anchorage

**ALASKA
(U.S.A.)**

*Chukchi
Sea*

Rocky Mountains

Yukon

*Wrangel
Island*

*East
Siberian
Sea*

Verkhoyansk Range

Lena

*Beaufort
Sea*

*New
Siberia
Islands*

○ Yellowknife

*Laptev
Sea*

*Victoria
Island*

*Queen
Elizabeth
Islands*

+ *North
Magnetic Pole*

*Severnaya
Zemlya*

CANADA

A R C T I C

+ *North Pole*

O C E A N

*Ellesmere
Island*

*Kara
Sea*

Yenisey

*Baffin
Island*

*Franz
Josef
Land*

*Baffin
Bay*

*Novaya
Zemlya*

Ob

Davis Strait

GREENLAND
(Denmark)

*Svalbard
(Norway)*

Ural Mountains

○ Yekaterinburg

*Barents
Sea*

RUSSIA

Godthab ■

○ Murmansk

*Greenland
Sea*

○ Arkhangelsk

Reykjavik ■

*Norwegian
Sea*

Arctic Circle

FINLAND

○ Nizhniy
Novgorod

ICELAND

*Faroe
Islands
(Denmark)*

SWEDEN

Helsinki ■

ESTONIA

Moscow ■

Key to Arctic map

■ Capital city
○ Major city or town
── Border (where one country joins another one)
── River
▨ Coast

ATLANTIC

OCEAN

NORWAY

Oslo ■ ■ **Stockholm**

LATVIA

*Baltic
Sea*

LITHUANIA

RUSSIA

BELARUS

*North
Sea*

DENMARK

IRELAND

**UNITED
KINGDOM**

NETHERLANDS

GERMANY

POLAND

UKRAINE

BELGIUM

**CZECH
REPUBLIC**

SLOVAKIA

MOLDOVA

ROMANIA

The Antarctic

The Antarctic, also called Antarctica, is the continent at the South Pole. It is the coldest and windiest continent. The land is covered with ice over 2,000m (6,500ft) thick. Nine-tenths of all the world's ice is in the Antarctic.

The Antarctic is at the bottom of the Earth. It is surrounded by the Southern Ocean.

This scientist is studying an ice cave. The cave is in an ice shelf, about 100m (328ft) thick, that floats on the sea.

Home for scientists

People started exploring the Antarctic just over 100 years ago. The only people who live there today are scientists. They study the weather, ice and rocks to try to find out more about life on Earth.

Keeping warm

The Antarctic is home to thousands of penguins. They have layers of fat underneath their feathers to protect them from the cold, and huddle together in big groups for extra warmth. Penguins take turns standing at the edge of the group, where it's windy and much colder.

Internet link

For a link to a website featuring Antarctic maps, satellite views, animals and even jokes go to **www.usborne-quicklinks.com**

SOUTHERN OCEAN

South Georgia
(U.K.)

South Sandwich
Islands
(U.K.)

Antarctic Circle

South Orkney Islands
(U.K.)

South Shetland Islands
(U.K.)

Queen Maud Land

Antarctic Peninsula

Weddell Sea

Coats Land

Enderby Land

ANTARCTICA

Ronne Ice Shelf

East Antarctica

Bellingshausen Sea

Ellsworth Land

Vinson Massif
5,140m
(16,863ft)

Transantarctic Mountains

+ South Pole

West Antarctica

Amundsen Sea

Marie Byrd Land

Ross Ice Shelf

Wilkes Land

Ross Sea

Victoria Land

South Magnetic Pole +

Antarctic Circle

SOUTHERN OCEAN

Scale

| 0km | 1,000km |
| 0 miles | 620 miles |

Key to Antarctic map

▲ Mountain

▬ Coast

This emperor penguin chick is keeping warm by standing on its mother's feet and snuggling up against her tummy.

Flags of the world

North America

Antigua and Barbuda

Bahamas

Barbados

Belize

Canada

Costa Rica

Cuba

Dominica

Dominican Republic

El Salvador

Grenada

Guatemala

Haiti

Honduras

Jamaica

Mexico

Nicaragua

Panama

St. Kitts and Nevis

St. Lucia

St. Vincent and the Grenadines

Trinidad and Tobago

United States of America

South America

Argentina

Bolivia

Brazil

Chile

Colombia

Ecuador

Guyana

Paraguay

Peru

Surinam

Uruguay

Venezuela

Asia

Afghanistan

Armenia

Azerbaijan

Bahrain

Bangladesh

Bhutan

Brunei

Burma (Myanmar)

Cambodia

China

East Timor

Georgia

Asia (continued)

India

Indonesia

Iran

Iraq

Israel

Japan

Jordan

Kazakhstan

Kuwait

Kyrgyzstan

Laos

Lebanon

Malaysia

Maldives

Mongolia

Nepal

North Korea

Oman

Pakistan

Philippines

Qatar

Russian Federation

Saudi Arabia

Singapore

South Korea

Sri Lanka

Syria

Taiwan

Tajikistan

Thailand

Turkey

Turkmenistan

United Arab Emirates

Uzbekistan

Vietnam

Yemen

Africa

Algeria

Angola

Benin

Botswana

Burkina Faso

Burundi

Cameroon

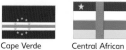
Cape Verde

Central African Republic

Chad

Comoros

Congo

Congo (Democratic Republic)

Djibouti

Egypt

Equatorial Guinea

Eritrea

Ethiopia

55

Africa (continued)

Gabon

The Gambia

Ghana

Guinea

Guinea-Bissau

Ivory Coast

Kenya

Lesotho

Liberia

Libya

Madagascar

Malawi

Mali

Mauritania

Mauritius

Morocco

Mozambique

Namibia

Niger

Nigeria

Rwanda

Sao Tome and Principe

Senegal

Seychelles

Sierra Leone

Somalia

South Africa

Sudan

Swaziland

Tanzania

Togo

Tunisia

Uganda

Zambia

Zimbabwe

Europe

Albania

Andorra

Austria

Belarus

Belgium

Bosnia and Herzegovina

Bulgaria

Croatia

Cyprus

Czech Republic

Denmark

Estonia

Finland

France

Germany

Greece

Hungary

Iceland

Europe (continued)

Ireland

Italy

Latvia

Liechtenstein

Lithuania

Luxembourg

Macedonia

Malta

Moldova

Monaco

Netherlands

Norway

Poland

Portugal

Romania

Russian Federation

San Marino

Serbia and Montenegro

Slovakia

Slovenia

Spain

Sweden

Switzerland

Turkey

Ukraine

United Kingdom

Vatican City

Oceania

Australia

Federated States of Micronesia

Fiji

Kiribati

Marshall Islands

Nauru

New Zealand

Palau

Papau New Guinea

Samoa

Solomon Islands

Tonga

Tuvalu

Vanuatu

Changing flags

Flags of the world change frequently. New flags are invented as new countries are born, or their situation changes.

For example, in 1991, there were important changes to the way South Africa was run. All adults in the country were allowed to vote in free elections for the first time. To celebrate this, a new flag was designed.

New flag of South Africa

South African flag until 1994

Internet links

For a link to a website with flags and facts, go to **www.usborne-quicklinks.com**

57

Map index

This is an index of all the places and features named on the maps. Each entry may contain the following parts: the name of the country, place or feature (in **bold** type), the country or region where a place or feature is (in *italic* type), and the page(s) where it can be found (in plain type). Some names also have a description explaining exactly what kind of place they are, for example, capital cities or rivers.

58

59

Index

Acknowledgements

Every effort has been made to trace the copyright holders of the material in this book. If any rights have been omitted, the publishers offer to rectify this in any future edition, following notification. The publishers are grateful to the following organizations and individuals for their contribution and permission to reproduce this material.

Cover (Front) Digital Vision, (back) Digital Vision; **1** NASA/Science Photo Library; **2–3** Getty Images/Pal Hermansen; **5** Getty Images/Walter Bibikow; **7** Getty Images/Louise Murray; **8**(b) Dave G. Houser/CORBIS; **14**(bl) Digital Vision; **15**(tr) Julian Baum & David Angus/Science Photo Library; **16**(l) Getty Images/John Giustina; **16–17** Getty Images/Macduff Everton; **17**(tr) Roger Ressmeyer/CORBIS; **18** Powerstock; **19**(tr) Owaki-Kulla/CORBIS, (l) Bryan & Cherry Alexander Photography/Alamy, (br) Getty Images/Doug Armand; **20**(bl) Digital Vision; **21**(tr) Julian Baum & David Angus/Science Photo Library; **22** Galen Rowell/CORBIS; **23**(tl) Powerstock, (r) Owen Franken/CORBIS, (bl) Robert Harding Picture Library Ltd/Alamy; **24** Jim Zuckerman/Alamy; **25**(r) Robert Harding Picture Library Ltd/Alamy, (l) Getty Images/Ary Diesendruck; **26**(bl) Digital Vision; **27**(tr) Julian Baum & David Angus/Science Photo Library; **28**(l) Jon Arnold Images/Alamy, (br) Michael S. Lewis/CORBIS; **29** Zefa/Masterfile/Miles Ertman; **30**(main) World Pictures, (bl) Macduff Everton/CORBIS; **31**(br) Powerstock; **33**(tr) Tom Van Sant/Geosphere Project, Santa Monica/Science Photo Library, (br) Digital Vision; **34–35**(b) Getty Images/Frans Lemmens; **35**(tr) Getty Images/Nick Garbutt, (m) NHPA/Daryl Balfour; **36** Dallas and John Heaton/Alamy; **37**(tr) Getty Images/Bruno De Hogues, (bl) Getty Images/Stephen Beer; **38**(ml) Digital Vision; **39**(br) Julian Baum & David Angus/Science Photo Library; **40**(bl) Art Kowalsky/Alamy; **40–41**(main) Jon Arnold Images/Alamy; **41**(mr) Getty Images/Wilfried Krecichwost; **42**(main) Getty Images/John Lawrence, (mr) Getty Images/Jorg Greuel; **43**(t) Powerstock, (bl) Getty Images/A & L Sinibaldi; **45**(t) Planetary Visions Ltd/Science Photo Library, (b) Digital Vision; **46**(b) Jean Paul Ferrero/Ardea London Ltd; **47**(t) Tim McKenna/CORBIS, (br) Theo Allofs/CORBIS; **48**(t) Mark A. Johnson/CORBIS, (br) Anders Ryman/CORBIS; **49**(ml) Jon Arnold Images/Alamy, (r) Wolfgang Kaehler/CORBIS; **50**(b) W. Perry Conway/CORBIS; **52** Graham Neden, Ecoscene/CORBIS; **53**(br) Tim David/CORBIS; **54–57** © Flag Institute Enterprises Ltd.

American editor: Carrie A. Armstrong